ISBN 960-7930-13-4

© Siphano, 1997 for the text and illustrations
Published in the UK by Siphano Picture Books 1999

UK edition text edited by Charles Bloom
Printed in Italy by Grafiche AZ, Verona

UK Edition distributed by RAGGED BEARS Ltd.,
Ragged Appleshaw, Hampshire, SP11 9HX, England
Tel: 44 (0)1264 772269 Fax: 44 (0)1264 772391e-mail: books@ragged-bears.co.uk

Mr. Cuckoo

BECKY BLOOM

SIPHANO PICTURE BOOKS

When Mr. Cuckoo came to live in the forest, the other animals asked him what he could do to earn a living.

"I can tell the time," replied Mr. Cuckoo proudly.

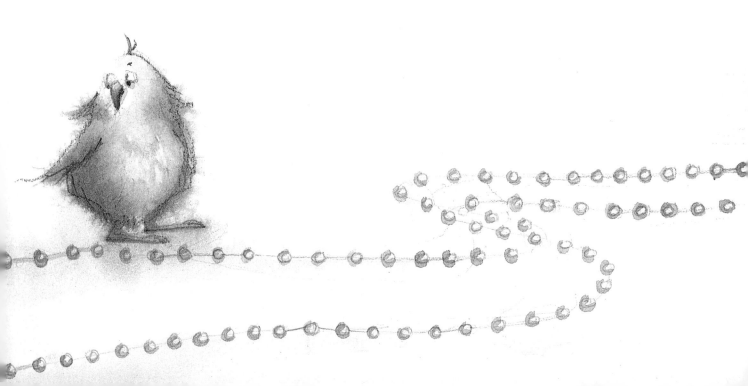

Mr. Cuckoo set to work at once, and soon
a beautiful little house stood in the middle of the forest.

Day and night, rain or shine, Mr. Cuckoo called out
the time. He chanted the hours, the quarters-past,
the halves-past and quarters-to, just as he had
pledged...

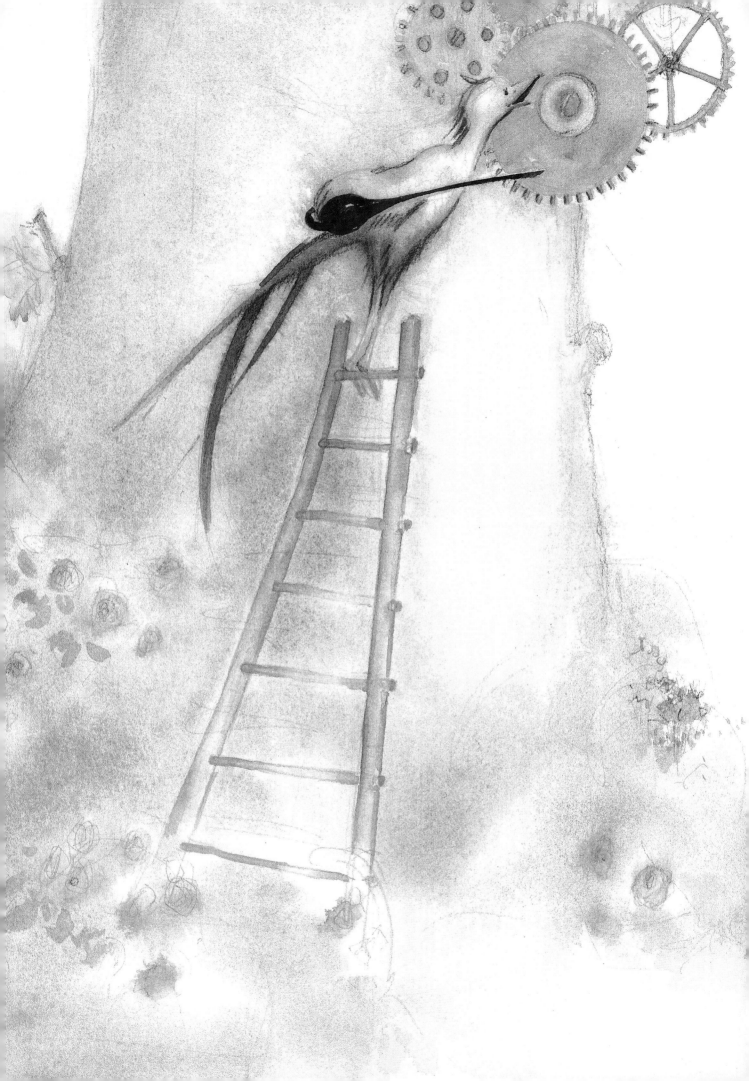

...and when he was not busy cuckooing,
he would oil the chains and gears of his clock,
clean the windows and shutters of his house
and water the roses that grew in his garden.

The animals of the forest were deeply
impressed.
If only they could be like Mr. Cuckoo!

Before long, knowing what time it was became very important to the animals of the forest. They all dreaded being late.

They carefully wrote their appointments
in tiny books and even the very youngest
animals had to learn difficult words like
schedule and *punctuality*.

The forest had changed but no one noticed. No one had time to!

Then one day, a fair girl Cuckoo came
to the forest. Mr. Cuckoo presented her
with a rose from his garden and
as she smelled it timidly, Mr. Cuckoo
stared at her.

Mr. Cuckoo stared for just a second,
or so it seemed to him. But hour
after hour went by, and Mr. Cuckoo forgot
to cuckoo the time. He missed
the quarters-past, the halves-past and
the quarters-to...

...until night fell
and the stars came out
and all the animals gathered
around Mr. Cuckoo's house
to see what had gone wrong.

But nothing was wrong. Mr. Cuckoo
was still staring at the beautiful girl
Cuckoo who kept smelling
her rose and looking at him
timidly from time to time.
So the animals thought
it was wise to simply
leave them alone and
they tip-toed back to their homes.

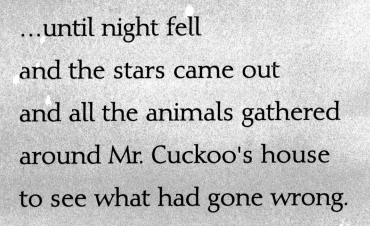

There weren't any more cuckoo chants
in the forest after that day
but the forest animals
did not mind at all.
Now they had time to realize
how much happier
they were.

And Mr. Cuckoo was the happiest of all....

Not long afterwards five Cuckoo chicks hatched
and everyone in the forest stopped by to admire them
and bring them presents.

No one chants the hours, the quarters-past, the halves-past and the quarters-to in the forest anymore.

But as the Cuckoo family grows bigger and noisier, bedtime stories in the forest often end like this:

Listen how quiet it is! The Cuckoo chicks must be in bed. It's time for you to go to bed, too.